## CHAPTER 1
## GRANDPAS MAP

*Sam walked down the creek bed looking for what ever sign he could find of the lost treasure he had read about. Not even sure he was in the right place he could only go by the maps he found in his gran paw papers. His grandpa had passed away and left him everything he had that wasn't a lot but*

Sam didn't mind. He cam up on the books in a old file cabinet and remembered the stories his grandpa had told him until now he thought they were just stories but the one map he found looked old as time he looked up toward heaven as to say I'll give it a shot grandpa. As he walked down the creek bed he stop to check the map and he looked ahead there he seen the over hang bluff on the map he thought could this map be real could all the stories his grandpa told him be real it was looking that way. He followed the creek till he came to a bend and seen a large Boulder high up on the bank he checked his map and there it was right on the map he walked over to the Boulder and seen carvings in the rock a arrow pointing down the creek Sam had come this far and he was planning to fallow the map till the end. As he worked his way farther down the creek he stopped to check the map somewhere up ahead there should be a large bluff but so far he had not seen one. By this time SAM was getting tired he had not plan to be gone this long he hadn't brought Any food or anything for camping out over night so he decided he would head home and get better supplies from the way this map was looking this could take a few days and he wanted to be prepared. As he walked along he wondered what the treasure would hold would there be gold and silver maybe jewelry it was hard telling. He looked up and seen the lights of town in the distant and was glad to see them by this time Sam was mighty hungry and tired.

## CHAPTER 2
## GEARING UP

Sam made it back to his house and went inside he thought to himself I need to plan this out a little better. Sam fixed him some supper and ate after he had finished he walked out to his shed and found his tent and sleeping bag. He walked back in the house and got his back pack and packed his tent and sleeping he thought I'll pack some food in the morning besides he was wore out he walked in his bedroom and climbed in to bed and drifted off to sleep. Next morning Sam got up and packed him enough supplies to last a few days he walked in to his gun cabinet and took out his 22 rifle and picked up a box of shells and put them in his pocket. Sam walked back in to the living room and picked up his backpack and put it on he walked out of the house and noticed a rope by the shed and thought I better take a rope it may come in handy he picked it up and placed it in the backpack then headed back up toward the woods. He walked till he came to *the last place that he was the day before then set down and studied the map after a while he took off again he had to find the big bluff there should be a trail the went along the top leading over the top after about a hour of walking he looked up head and could see a huge bluff reaching up high he thought that must be it it was around thousand yards ahead. It was getting toward evening when Sam reached the foot of the bluff he thought this would be a perfect place to camp for tonight so he unpack his back pack and put up the tent next to some cedar trees then he collected some firewood for the night. After Sam got a fire going he cooked him some food for supper the he settled in for the night. As he set around the camp fire he thought this must be how it felt to the old ones who came before so peaceful. Sam set a listen to coyotes barking of in the night till he became tired then he climbed in to his tent and called it a night.*

## CHAPTER 3
## THE NEXT DAY

*Next morning Sam got up and poured him some water in a pot a fixed him some coffee the made him a fast breakfast. He ate the packed up his gear and started his day he seen off just a short walk was a trail going up the side of bluff. He made it half way up* the trail and it became narrow and wore down from the weather he clung close to the edge more then once he thought of turning back he knew if he slipped it would be over so he watched ever step knowing it could be his last. When he got close to the top he breathed a si of relief to have that climb behind him he climbed up over the rocks on top and came to a flat rock top he set down and took out the map and checked it looking for his next sign he would need to go down hill till he come a creek then he would walk for what it looked for a long way till he came to a wood lot. So he took of walking again down off the top of the bluff down toward the creek *at the bottom. After half of day walking he got to thinking this creek can't be much farther then he heard a squirrel barking in the distant then he seen the edge of the creek and this raised his spirits Sam was tired from the long walk and was ready to get something to eat. Sam reach the creak about sunset and gathered some firewood then put his tent up and cooked him some supper after awhile of setting around the fire he crawled in his tent wore out from the day he drifted off to sleep. Next morning Sam got up thinking I sure hope I find the cave at the end of this map today I'm running out of supplies and need to be getting back* home he fixed coffee and breakfast and studied the map then realized he was pretty close to where he needed to be. Sam packed up all his gear and started walking south from the creek where came to a gulch he walked about two hundred yards when he seen a small cave he walked up toward the cave and it opened to a larger cave. Sam became excited he made it to the cave he set up his tent and gathered firewood then set down for some lunch he looked at the map and seen some markings by the cave symbol so he finished his lunch then took a walk to the cave he took his 22 rifle just in case of danger. At the entrance to the cave he found markings

just like the map said Sam looked up
toward heaven and said it's real
grandpa I found the cave. Sam check
the walls for more signs and came
across some more carvings and
followed them back in to the cave he
turned on his flashlight and walked
further back till he seen where the cave
was turning he shined the flashlight
down on the map then back in to the
cave and he seen a rock ledge he
walked five steps off end of the ledge
and stopped and looked at the floor of
the cave he seen a low spot and dug till
he hit something hard he shine the light
and seen the lid of what looked to be a
old box he open it and found a box full

*of high grade gold ore he couldn't believe his eyes. Sam thought to himself where did all this gold ore come from there must be thousands of dollars in the box he shined he light to the back of the cave and caught the flicker of something he walked back and there in the wall was gold big vain of gold running in the walls Sam was rich he thought I need to get back and file a gold claim on this sight then he thought how am I going to pack all this gold ore out he would need a horse to get in this back country. He thought to him self I'll cover this gold back up and get some rest and head back in morning to file a gold claim then he* could work this claim. He walked back out of the cave and started his campfire then settled in for the night.

## CHAPTER 4
### GOLD CLAIM

Sam got up next morning had a good breakfast and headed back home early he was going to try to make it home by dark he new it would be a long day. He came to the bluff and started back down and by a little after sun down he made it to the house wore out he walked in to the house and left his backpack by the door grabbed a bite to eat and climbed in bed. Sam was up early the next day had a good breakfast and went to town to file his claim he got *that all taken care of then he stopped at his friend Jim's house he walked up to the house and Jim came out to met him he said hello Sam what can I do for you Sam said I need to talk a little business deal with you Jim see if you might be interested. Jim said so tell me all about it Sam said we'll you know I told you about the map my grandpa left me Jim said I remember your grandpa was a good old timer but I doubt if that maps real Sam just smiled and said Jim it's real I found the cave. Jim said are you sure Sam said I'm very sure it's a gold mine and I want to make you my partner in it you got horses and pack animals to get our gold ore out I know you been having some hard times so thought I'd ask you first Jim said we'll I sure would Sam said we'll I filed claim this morning but if you want let's go back down there and I'll add your name to it Jim said let's go. Sam said I was hoping you would say yes I know you have experience in mining Jim said I could sure use the work they both walked out and got in his truck and drove down to the claims office and added Jim's name to claim then they went back to Jim's. Sam said we're going to need some supplies for a week and tools Jim said I got 4 good pack mules and horses to ride and all the tool we will need Sam said that's great.*

*They walked out Jim open the doors on his shed and took out picks and shovels and rock hammers Sam said you got everything don't you Jim said we'll not everything but a lot he got all the tools and took them up to his porch Jim turned to Sam and said I'll pack up all my supplies and you go get the grub we will need and we will leave at daylight in the morning Sam said sounds good to me Jim said I have a big cabin tent that will be a lot more comfortable to live in Sam said that sounds good I'll be here before daylight tomorrow and we will take off I'll go pick up some food now and see you in the morning.*

# CHAPTER 5
# THE RIDE IN

*Sam was up early the next morning and at Jim's house before day light when he pulled in his headlights shined on Jim loading his mules Jim waved and said bring the food here and I'll pack the mules. Sam carried the goods over and set them down while Jim packed mules and spread the weight out even making it easier on the mules. After few minutes all there supplies was loaded and Jim said I guess that's it Sam noticed Jim was packing his Ruger black hawk Sam said yep I guess that's it and the climbed up on there horses and took off with the pack mules coming along behind it looked like a scene from a old western as they went down the side road. They rode through the end of town till they came to the end of town Jim said where did you say this cave was Sam said it's in Badger gulch Jim said I know a better way around the bluff to get there Sam say that's good with me cause he had no idea how he would get the horse up the bluff. Then came to a field at the end of town and Jim took point and lead across the field till they came to the first creek the horses stepped down the bank wadding across the creek and*

came up the bank on the other side.
Sam seen the big bluff off to his left and
Jim stayed to the right after couple
hours of riding they came to the second
creek and followed it till they came to
the area of the came Jim said I'll let you
led in sense you know where the cave
is Sam said OK as he brought his horse
around up front before long they came
to the mouth of the cave and Sam
looked back and said here we are he
climbed down off his horse and tied
him off to a small tree Jim climbed
down and said I'll get ten set up then
we can unload our gear and supplies
Sam said sounds like a plan before
long they had the tent setup and Jim

*and Sam unloaded the supplies in to the tent Jim carried in a couple cots Sam looked over and said we'll Alright that's going to be nice to have a bed to sleep in Jim walked the horses and mules over to a grass area and tied them off then he came walking back he reach in the tent and pulled our a couple lawn chairs and said I'm ready to set for minute. Sam said I'll get a fire going and fix us something to eat then I'll show you the claim Jim said sounds like a plan. Sam got a good fire going and fried up some spam and beans after awhile they ate Sam told Jim when we're done ill show you what I found in the claim Jim said what you found Sam* said yes while I was in the claim I found some symbols so I checked it out and found something buried. Jim said what did you find Sam said we'll you will just have to wait and see it. He finished up there dinner then Sam said if your ready I'll show you the inside of the claim. Jim said I'm ready and Sam said let me grab us some lights .

## CHAPTER 6

## THE BIG SURPRISE

Sam came back from the tent and handed Jim a flash light and said let's go check it out they walked toward the cave. As they entered the cave Jim said tomorrow I'll get some proper lighting set up in here Sam said how we going to do that Jim said you know that big flat box you put in tent Sam said yes Jim said that has solar panels in it and solar lights that we will run along the ceiling of the cave. Sam said we'll ain't that something that will make it so much better. As the went farther in the mine Sam came to the ledge he walked to where he had covered up the box and stopped and bent down and started to uncover the box till he could see the lid. Jim bent down and said we'll what do we have here same said this is what I was telling you about. Sam reach down and open the lid on the box and reached in and took a hold of a chunk of the gold ore and handed it to Jim he

shine his light on it and looked back up
at Sam and said can we get this box out
of here so I can check it out better in
the sunlight Sam said sure Jim tossed
the ore back in the box and they dug
around the box till they could move it
then each one of them grabbed a side
and lifted it out of the ground and set it
back down on the out side of the hole.
Jim shined his light in the hole and said
Sam there is another box in that hole
Sam quickly shine his light in the hole
and said what would they do this Jim
said it's a ore stash it's where they hid
it till they could come back to get it and
from the looks of that old box it's been
in the ground a very long time. Let's

*take this box out and we can come back for the other one later Sam said OK and they reached down and carried the box out of the cave in to the sunlight. They set down in there chairs and Jim took his jewelries loop out of his pocket and raised the lid on the box and took out a chunk of ore he held the ore in his hand turning it around as he looked through the loop then he looked back at Sam and said this is some of the riches high grade ore I've ever seen where rich Sam were rich Sam jumped up and hey danced all around with excitement Jim had gone his hole life with out having much of anything working his hands raw and Sam had*

*done the same now it was all going to
pay off. Jim walked over to the tent and
took a small tarp out of a bag and
spread it out on the ground and he said
help me pour this box out on this tarp
Sam said OK they poured it out and the
gold in the ore shined in the  sunlight.
This was more riches then the both had
ever seen in there lifetime Sam said you
reckon that other box has ore in it to
Jim said we will never know unless we
did it up Sam said we'll let's get this
back in the box and go dig the other
one up.*

## CHAPTER 7
## MOTHER LODE

*They set the box in side the big tent and covered it with a saddle blanket then they walked back out and toward the mine and back till they came to where the box was buried. Sam said you hold the light Jim and I'll dig he dug till he had the box uncovered then he said we'll that's about it Jim laid the flashlight down and the both reached down and grabbed a hold of the box it was so heavy much heavier then the other box they looked at each other then Jim said wonder why this box is so heavy Sam said I don't know but we need to get it out Jim said maybe we can unload some of it take some weight out of it so they tried to pry the top off but it wouldn't budge Sam said we'll let's try to lift it out again Jim said OK he both grabbed a hold of the box and they lifted and pulled till they felt it move then it came loose and the lifted with all they had till the box came out of the hole. They set it down on the mine floor and rested for awhile both were curious what was so heavy in the box Jim said I got a idea let's cut a couple poles and tie the box to them it will be a lot easier to lift Sam said great idea. Sam went out of the mine and got his saw and cut two beach poles and took them back in the mine. Jim fastened them to the box and looked up at Sam and said that should do it they each* grabbed a end of the poles and raised the box up and out of he mine they went they set it down in front of there chairs and both took a seat and rested Sam said I don't know about you Jim but I won't to see what's in that box Jim said I'm with you and he walked in he tent and got a pry bar and hammer and came back out he drove the flat bar under the wood on top and payed down with all he had the lid raised up and Jim moved the bar to the other side and pushed down on the bar and the lid popped loose they both looked at each other. Sam reached and raised the lid and there on the top was something wrapped in wax paper Sam picked it up and unwrapped it and there in his hand was a walker colt he looked at it for a minute then handed it to Jim he said we'll would you look at that that gives you a idea of how long this gold ore been in the ground this is from late 1800s Sam said yes its been in there awhile. Then they took a old news paper off the top and underneath it was something they had not expected in the box laid nicely stacked Confederate gold bars stacked to the top both men just stared in disbelief Jim looked at Sam and said is that real Sam said I sure hope so Jim took one of the bars from the box and held it in his hand it was so heavy. Sam said those bars *must weight 40 pounds a piece Jim looked up and said no they weight 50 pounds I read up a lot on this subject were millionaires my God were so Richie need to dig a hold and put this in it to keep it safe till we leave for home Sam said I agree Sam picked up the old news paper it was yellow from age and faded he seen at he top May 4 1865 he handed it to Jim and pointed to the date Jim smiled and said we're holding history in our hands. Sam said let's dig a hole a put his in it in case someone happens to come by Jim said I'll help they went to back of tent wracked back the leaves and started the hole when they were finished the came back and put the lid back on the box and fixed the poles to it and  carried it around and placed it in the hole they laid the poles to the side they covered the box and covered it back with the leaves to blend it back in then they made a promise that each will protect the gold never telling where it was for anything they both agreed. They carried the poles back around to the side of the tent then they both set down in there chairs Jim said I need a drink Sam said me to Jim reached in his saddle bag and pulled out a bottle of whiskey he twisted the lid of handed it to Sam and he took a big drink handed it back to Jim he turned the bottle up and took a* big drink then he looked back at Sam and said you know we don't even have to mine hat gold those gold bars are enough for both of us for life Sam said yes but don't you think people we'll wonder where we got that kind of money if we work that mine that covers up the gold we just melt it down with the gold ore and know one will ever know Jim looked up and smiled and said that's a beautiful idea they both swore to never speak a word of it.

## CHAPTER 8
## WORKING THE MINE

Sam got up and said I better fetch some wood for the fire tonight or we won't have one Jim said I'll help the got up *and walked off in the woods and before long they had enough wood for a few days. Jim said I better tend to horses and mules Sam said I'll give you a hand the walked them down the short distance to the creek and let him drink there fell then walked them back Jim tied a rope between two trees and and tied the horses and mules to it and they both walked back to there camp by this time it was starting to get dark Sam said I reckon I'll start a fire before long he had a nice fire going and Jim said I could eat a bite how about you Sam said yes I could how's chili sound Jim said sounds good to me Sam said I got a whole bag of cornbread to have with it Jim said I can't wait . Sam walked in tent and got the cast iron bean pot and brought it out  and got the chili going then he got some water and put it in the coffee pot and got them some coffee going. Before they both were eating chili Sam handed Jim the bag of cornbread they both had a big supper and set by the fire drinking coffee and listening to the night critters Jim said this is truly the good life Sam said it sure is so peaceful up hear a man could get used to living like this. Jim said I'll start string he light in the cave in the morning so we can see a lot better I think we should put the solar panels on the slope over there I noticed the sun hits there most of the day I got two batteries that should be enough to run some lights Sam said sounds great you know I never really thought about the lights I'm glad you did Jim said after we get lights hooked up we can tell better off what we got to work with. Sam I tell you what I'm about wore out I'm ready to hit the sack Jim said me to and they both called it a night. Next morning they got up early and Sam fixed breakfast and a big pot of coffee they set and ate and talked of plans for the day after they were finished Jim walked over to his tool bag and took out his drill and 6 batteries he set he charger in the sun and Sam noticed it had a solar panel on the top of it Sam thought to himself that's pretty cool Jim walked back in the tent and brought out the big bag with the solar panels in it he took them out of the bag and then he reach in and took a roll of wire and a bag of lights he had twenty six volt lights Sam picked up one of the lights and looked at it Jim said them are lithium lights there real bright and don't use much power Sam said just what we need. Jim said I could sure use your help hooking these up Sam said anything you need just let me know. Jim said OK let's get started he picked up the roll of wire and they walked to the entrance of the mine Jim took out his drill it had a long masonry bit he drill a hole up toward the top of mine and place a hanger in the hole every twenty feet he drilled a hole and placed a hanger then he walked back out and pulled the wire through the hangers till he came to the last one deep in the mine. Then he picked up the bag of lights and they went deep in the mine and started with the last on and hooked them up one by one till they were at the entrance of the mine again Jim drilled a hole about eye level and placed a light switch and hooked the wires to it then ran the wire outside the cave to where he had place the batteries and cut the wire just long enough to hook up then he walked over to where he had put the solar panels he got hem set up at the right angle then he ran the wires back to to the batteries and hooked them up then he hooked he end for the lights to the batteries after a minute he said we'll Sam hit the switch Sam flipped the switch and the cave lit up bright they walked back inside and were amazed how good hey could see. You could see the veins of gold running through he wall the walls were full of gold reaching out in different directions. They both new it was going to be a lot of work but they were ready to get it started Jim said when we're not in the mine we shut the light out that let's the batteries stay charged. Sam said I think we got enough supplies for about a week then one of us can go get more supplies while the other watches the mine Jim agreed.*


## CHAPTER 9
## START MINEING

*Jim ask Sam do you want to spend rest of the day checking out the mine maybe even working some of the gold out Sam said I thought you would never ask. The walked over to the mine and flipped the switch Sam turn to Jim you know I all most for got we need to post are mine papers one the corners of our claim best way is to nail a jar to a tree and put paper in jar screw it back in. Jim said you think we can do it in morning Sam said oh yeah that will be fine. They walked in to  the mine and walked to the back checking the gold in the back vain Sam said thus vain here seems to be the biggest and most likely to produce Jim walked over and checked it out and said I believe your right Sam this vain looks real good won't really know how good till we get in to it Sam said we'll let's get in to it. They walked out and got there picks and shovels and other tools the thought they might need they walked back in to the mine and to the back where the ore vain was in the wall. Jim  grabbed his pick and* started swinging at the vain chip by chip he worked I'll after awhile he had worked a nice pile of ore out he stopped and looked at Sam and said we really need a wheelbarrow Sam said yes we do Sam said when we go in town for supplies we will get one Jim sad well hat will just be a few more days while I'm in town I'll bring something to blast to walls out I have half of a case of dynamite that I will bring it will make life a lot easier I got a masonry bit that I can drill the holes with save us a lot of back breaking work Sam said that sounds great I can't wait. Sam bent over and gathered up some of the better looking ore and *placed it in a bucket then carried it out of the mine Jim came along behind him and they both looked through the bucket Jim said I have to say this is some of the riches ore I've ever seen. We need to to feel up those floor sacks I brought so when I go back in we can take and load out to have it crushed and tested Sam agreed Jim walked in the tent a brought out some heavy duty floor sacks and Sam said OK well let's fill them up. Jim said what we need is a rock crusher Sam said that would sure be nice they took the bucket of ore and poured it in the floor sack then they brought the box of ore out and filled the sack up and tied it off. After three more days of mining it came time to go back in to town Jim said I'll get up in the morning and load the mules and that way I'll be back before sundown Sam said OK I'll get up early and get started loading them .*

## CHAPTER 10
## TRIP TO TOWN

*They were up at sun up and fixed breakfast and coffee then they started loading the mules they got all the ore bags strapped on to the mules then Jim said is there anything else you can think of Sam said no just what we put on list Jim said OK I'll run by and drop ore off to be crushed then I'll go get some supplies is there anything you need from your house Sam said know I'm good Jim said OK then I guess I better get started Jim said I'll see you tonight Sam watched as Jim faded off in the distant then he walked back in the mine to work. Jim rode along for awhile when came off the hill he could see town in he distant as he came in to town he went by the assay office and didn't the paperwork and said I'll be back after awhile I got to get some supplies the man said it should all be done in 3 hours Jim said OK I'll be back later. Jim rode on down main street crossed to the end of town and stopped by his house to get he dynamite he packed it safe on he mule then went*

down by the supplies store he picked
up all the goods he needed he picked a
wheelbarrow and tied it on one of the
mules by this time a few hours had
gone by so Jim thought he would drop
back by the assay office. He walked
back in the office the man just looked at
Jim when he walked back in he said I
just finished up your order can I ask
you who name to put on your
paperwork Jim told him his and Sam's
name he old guy loomed back up and
said son I ain't never seen ore this rich
before do you mind telling me where it
came from Jim just looked at him and
said I can't do that loose lips sinks
ships the old guy just smiled and said

we'll here's your paperwork looks like your getting 5 oz a ton that's extremely rich ore I crushed all your ore about a ton it's 99.5 pure that's $7500 dollars in ore you fellas are setting on a very rich load mine Jim paid the man for his work and ask him if he knew a better way to get ore out other then mules the old man said son I been in this business a very long time I've seen all kinds of things people have tried but if your in back country mules about the only way to go. You know son you would save your self a lot of trouble if you had a rock crusher and a sluice you could crush on the spot and sluice the gold out then you wouldn't have to *mess with the trash rock it's taking you a lot to carry all that rock to town you need a rock crusher bad. The old man said I'll tell you what son I have a hand crank rock crusher I've had it for awhile Jim said how much does it weight the old man said I guess its about two hundred pounds but I have a old two wheel cart if the country isn't to rough you could haul it in it and I have a old sluice in good shape Jim said we'll the country ain't to rough what would something like that cost me the old man said we'll I'll tell you for you for sluice and rock crusher I'd let you have it for 500 dollars and I'd throw in he cart Jim looked at the old man and said that's fair deal I'll take it. The old man said good and son I've seen gold from all over this area and that gold you got is the purest I've ever seen there only one area that has gold that has it that pure that would be Badger gulch but that mine hasn't been worked sense late 1800s I know cause my grandfather worked that mine Jim just smiled and said maybe the old man said your safe with me son. Jim handed the old man 500 dollars and they walked out to the shed out back he hooked the cart to his strongest mule then loaded the rock crusher in the back the old man walked in and carried out part of the sluice and told Jim there's another half in side its*

*12 foot put together you set this up down stream and hook this water line to it and run it up stream and gravity does the rest. Jim said thank you so much for everything and I'll be back in couple weeks and we will do some more business the old man said by he way my name is Bill but my friends call me smokey cause I like to smoke a pipe lol Jim said smokey I'll see you next trip in and he shook smokey hand and rode of toward the mine. Jim thought I must be quite a site with mules loaded down and a cart coming along behind after about 3 hours Jim come riding in to camp Sam waved his hands he was glad to see him.*

# CHAPTER 11
## SAMS BIG SURPRISE

Jim climbed down off his horse Sam said what in he world is that cart Jim smiled and said you like that Sam said it will come in hand to haul ore Jim said we'll that's what's in the back of cart it's a rock crusher Sam jumped up and ran over and look a it where in the world did you get that and a big sluice box and hose wow that's great Sam was talking so fast Jim couldn't get a word in. He looked at Sam and said so I guess you approve of my shopping spree laughed Sam said yes I do this will make it so much easier where did you get it. Jim said we'll I'll tell you all *about it but let get our supplies*

*unloaded first Sam said sure and they*

*started unloading Sam said you sure*

*got a lot of supplies this time Jim said*

*don't make know sense running to town*

*every week Sam said your right Sam*

*grabbed the last bag on mule Jim said*

*go easy with that dynamite Sam looked*

*at Jim and said I'll let you get that Jim*

*just laughed after they were unloaded*

*they unhooked the mule from trailer*

*Jim and Sam walked the horse and*

*mules down to the creek and watered*

*them Sam said so did everything go*

*good Jim said yep it went better then in*

*thought it would they walked back and*

*tied the horses and mules for the night*

*Jim said you no we really need to take a day a make the animals a corral Sam said that would be a great idea we could build one in short time we can do that tomorrow if you like Jim said sounds good Sam said come eat him I got a good beef stew on Jim said that sounds good they set down and Jim reached in his pocket and pulled the assay paperwork out and handed it to Sam he looked it up and down then looked up at Jim and said 5 oz a ton Jim smiled and yep he said it was extremely rich we made seven thousand five hundred I spent 500 hundred on he rock crusher sluice box and he through in cart Sam said are you serious that rock crusher would cost a couple thousand by its self you did real good my friend real good. Jim said now we can crush here and won't have to pack all that rock to town Sam said yep and I can't wait to get started. Sam said I got big pile chipped out today so after we get the corral done we can get it all set up Jim said sounds good to me. They both ate a big supper then set around enjoying the evening Jim walked in to he tent and come back out with a pint of wild turkey he open the lid and handed it to Sam he took a big drink then handed it back to Jim he turned it up and set down in his chair he said here's the money from the gold today seven thousand dollars  same reached out took the money counted out three thousand two hundred fifty dollars and handed the rest back to Jim and said there's your share I took out for my share on rock crusher Jim said we'll that's fair enough. They set and talked to way up in the night they both hit the hay. Next morning they were up early Sam made breakfast and then set and ate and drank coffee Jim said we're doing pretty good don't you think Sam. Sam looked up and said like you said Jim this gold prospecting is just a hobby now everything we make is just extra money that box in the ground is what it's all about for both of us Jim said your absolute right Sam we can both retire on just what's in that box but I'd like to be able to have enough to help some folks to Sam looked up and said yes me to I know a few people I'd love to help out Jim said and we will buddy when we're all done here. Jim got his axes and saw and walked over and cut down some trees about as big as his arm Sam came along behind him and cut the limbs off then through them in a pile after awhile Jim walked over got him a roll of wire and they started building the corral before long they had it all done a mice big corral Jim said this will be so much better on the animals we'll let's go get them they* walked the horses over and raised the log up and let the horses go in and then went and got the mules. Jim said I got a salt block for them when I was in town yesterday Sam said I bet they like that and sure enough they started licking on it right away Sam said it isn't even noon yet we got time to start setting up sluice Jim said let's do it they walked over and picked up the sluice box and carried it over to the creek then they walked back and got the other half  they put it together Sam looked up stream a noticed how the creek was a lot higher he said you know what I'm thinking Jim looked and said yep I sure do the run the water line up stream placed a rock on it and the water started running through the sluice it was the perfect set up Sam said now if we had that rock crusher set up here we could crush and feed it in to sluice box Jim said let do it. They built up the rocks level then set the rock crusher on top of it before long they were set up Sam couldn't wait to run some rocks through it they got the new wheelbarrow and loaded it up and placed there first rock in to he crusher it worked great crushing it up nice Jim said we need to build a hopper on that sluice box and set that rock crusher right on top of it Sam said I'm sure we could do it so they thought about it and

*and before long they had it all set up perfectly.*

## CHAPTER 12
## RUNNING THE SLUICE BOX

*They spent the rest of the day running ore through the sluice after awhile they started seeing gold show up on he riffles in the sluice that's when they new it was going to work just fine. They ran through all the ore they had then Jim said sounds like Time to brake out he dynamite I'll take my drill in to the mine and drill some holes and blow use enough ore out to last for awhile same said sounds good Jim said I'll drill the holes if you would like to clean the sluice out same said sounds good to me. Jim got his drill and walked in and after a few hours he had all the holes drilled he walked back out got the dynamite and loaded the holes then shut the lights off and took the bulbs out so the blast would break them. Sam came in and said how's it going Jim said just about ready to blast how did the clean out go Sam said take a guess Jim said I don't know Sam said four and half oz for less then a ton that's pretty darn good Jim said you aren't kidding that's good there's a lock box in the tent we can put it in Sam said OK I got it in a little bottle right now. Jim said well I'll take a look at it after I blast his. They walked back out of mine Jim said stay clear I'll be right back he walked in mine and come running back out fire in he hole . And they both got behind a tree then a big bang and rumble came from the mine followed by a lot of dust Jim said let let hat clear out then we will go back and check it out. Sam handed the bottle of gold to Jim and said what do you think Jim looked at it and very nice  we keep going we will feel that jar up in no time at all. After awhile Jim said we'll I suppose it's OK to see how the blast went they flipped the lights on and Jim carried the last two bulbs in and put hem back in place when the light shined out over the area Jim walked over to where he had loaded the holes and he looked back at Sam but Sam had all ready seen it there in front of them was a wall of gold everywhere they looked was gold they couldn't believe there eyes. Jim walked out and grabbed a pick and walked back in a started swinging at the wall huge chunks of gold fell to the floor Sam just looked and finally said my God what did we do to be so blessed Jim looked back at Sam and said there's more gold here then in that box we got buried Sam said you think Jim said oh yeah that's all most pure gold Jim reached down and picked a big piece and they walked back out of the mine. When the sunlight hit the ore in his hand Jim couldn't*

believe it it truly was almost pure gold
same got the wheelbarrow and shovel
and went back in to the mind and
loaded it full he came back out and Jim
walked over and looked in the
wheelbarrow Sam just stood and stared
in to the wheelbarrow all they could see
was the color gold looking back at them
Jim said is all that real Sam said it sure
is Jim said what are we going to do
with all this Sam said well we both said
we wanted to help some folks Jim said
let's get this in a bag it's starting to get
dark Sam said is something wrong Jim
said know it's just happening to fast do
you realize how much money talking
about Sam yes I know it's a lot to think

*about tell you what lets get some supper and set an relax the rest of the day Jim said that sounds like a good idea. Sam got a fire going and before long had supper on the stove they set and ate and Jim said we need to start taking gold in to town and store it in a safe place Sam said I agree you no that's something I been thinking about a lot Jim said next time I go in to town I'll take a big load in we need to find a real buyer the assay man hasn't got that kind of money it would take to buy a large amount of gold Sam said your right we need to get right on that pretty soon it won't be long and it will be fall so we need to find a buyer. Jim said let's run that ore from the blast and see what's behind the wall we just blasted Sam said our right I'll start running in he morning.*

## CHAPTER 13
## LOTS OF GOLD

*They set around the fire till late in to the night next morning after breakfast Sam started crushing ore early till he had run a hole wheelbarrow load Jim said there's another load in the mine Sam said I'm going to have to do a clean out first my riffles are full of gold Jim said OK I'll go get a load for you and you can do clean out Sam said OK I'll get started now. A couple hours later Jim walked back out and Sam said we did* pretty good Jim said how much Sam said right at 78 oz of gold out of one wheelbarrow Jim said you got to be kidding me Sam said know joking it's for real Jim said we'll let's run another load through it by the time dark came they had run 3 more loads of ore and collected another 567oz of gold Jim said this is unbelievable. Jim and Sam walked back in the mine and check the wall for tomorrow's work Sam said looks like it's getting thin Jim said that's what I'm thinking well we will see in morning. They went out to the fire Sam made a fast supper and Jim talk about what they would do in morning he said Sam it looks like that vain of *gold played out so we need to find another one if we can't find one we may have to call or trip short Sam said we'll we will know more tomorrow. It was getting late when Jim got up and said I believe I'll go to bed Sam said me to I'm wore out Sam laid there in his bed listening to the water in the creek and a old hoot owls in the distance he said you know Jim I'm sure going to miss this place when we go to leave Jim said yes me to this place grows on you its mighty peaceful here just think the old timers got to listen to this all the time Sam said yes I was born hundred years to late Jim said me to. Next morning they got up early and had breakfast and*

coffee then walked in o the mine the
checked several promising veins but
nothing seem to check out then Jim
found what might be a good vein he
drill holes and loaded the dynamite in
them he turned around and told Sam
let's get out of here and Blast this hole
out they got outside and Sam said I'm
going to light it stay clear he stepped
back In and lit it and ran back out he
got behind the tree and then came the
boom and dust rushed out of the mine
after hey had given the air time to clear
the walked in he mine and checked it
Jim said it not to bad its worth crushing
Sam said OK I'll get the wheelbarrow
and load it up after awhile he came

*back out of mine and and ran the ore through the sluice then went back to get another load by the time late afternoon came he decided to do a clean out he got it all done Jim said I was the clean out Sam said we'll we got 13 oz Jim said that's not bad don't let all those big clean outs ruin this a 13 oz clean out is super good Sam said I know your right Jim. After awhile Jim said we'll tomorrow is two weeks I better take a load in to town and get some supplies Sam why don't you come with me get out of here for awhile Sam said who's going to watch the camp Jim said there isn't no one going to bother anything Sam said we'll OK it*

*ain't like we will be gone long OK I'll go
Jim said good we will load up at
daylight and take off early.*

## CHAPTER 14
## THE BUYER

*Early next morning they loaded up the
mules Sam said Jim you think we
should take that bar gold in to your
place and store it Jim said I think that's
a great idea hat way won't worry about
it so much they hook the mule up to the
wagon and dug up the box of gold and
put it in he wagon. Loaded the mules
with the 798 oz of gold Jim said that
sure is a lot of money Sam said it sure
is they closed up the tent and headed
toward town three hours later they were*

*in town they went through town to Jim's house he said let's go out by the barn and he said let's bury it Sam laughed and said OK after they covered it up and blended the area in they went down toward the assay office Jim's dad was down town he hollered hey Jim where you been son Jim said been working a claim up in the hills are you doing any good Jim said I'll let you know later he said we'll you be careful and come by when you can Jim said I will they went on down till they came to the assay office the got off and tied up the horses and went inside. Jim walked in and said hey smokey he looked up and said well hello son how have you* been oh I been pretty good who do you got with you oh this is Sam my partner well hello Sam good to meet you so how did hat crusher work for you it did a great job I'm happy to here that so tell me I need to get rid of some gold smokey said how much we talking I'm in the market for some well I'm not sure you can handle what we got well let me know Jim looked at him and said we got just under 800 oz smokey said holy cow you boys have been working well I can't take all of it but I can take some off your hands I know another guy that can take the rest Jim said do you trust him smokey said yeah I trust him he's my brother smokey said I'll take about half of what you got . He pour he gold on the scale and weighted out 400 oz he said that will be right at 600 thousand if you like we can go to the bank and get a bank check or if you go a account I can transfer to your account Sam said we'll we both bank there so we can just transfer to out account are you OK with that Jim he said sure. Jim said can you weight what's left smokey said sure can he weighted it and said just hair under 498 oz Jim said you say your brother would want it smokey said let me call him and see. Smokey got off phone and said he will me us at the bank he will take it all that well be 748 thousand or 373 thousand 500 a piece

*Sam said sound good to me smokey said that claims paying big for you fellas. Well we better to get to he bank when they got there smokey brother was waiting he said hello fellas I'm Earl let's go in side they walked in side smokey seen the bank Manger and raised his hand and waved to come back he waved them back before long smokey and his brother had bought all there gold they all shook hands smokey said let me know when you get back next run in Sam said oh you can count on it. Smokey said you fellas didn't find anything else up there I mean here's a legion of a Confederate gold being buried up there but know one has ever found it Jim said we'll if a man found it how could he get rid of it I mean Don that state get part of it smokey said forget that state I don't deal with them I'd melt it down make small bars out of it Sam looked at Jim smokey and his brother looked at hem and said you found it didn't you Sam didn't say a word Jim looked at smokey and said I'll but it all off you Earl said I want half so tell me Jim are they 50lb or 20 lb bars Jim didn't say a word hey just smiled you know our grandfather worked that claim when he was a young man and he was killed there by his partner I'll just say if you do find it me and my brother will by every oz off you Jim said that's good to know if we find it we will get back to you smokey said I'm sure you will Sam and Jim went back to Jim's house Sam said what you think about smokey you think we can trust him Jim said I believe we can I think he just wants to have a part of his grandpa treasure he didn't say it but it's easy to read his face Sam said we'll I trust you Jim and and what ever you say is good with me Jim said I know that old man's got a lot of money if he wants to buy that cost we just put more money in our account then I've ever seen Sam yes your right Jim said let's just go talk to him see what he says Sam says OK let's go.*

## CHAPTER 15
## SELLING THE GOLD

*The rode back to smokey place and walked inside hen seen Earl was there to smokey looked and said that didn't take long what can I do for you fellas Jim said smokey we might of found something in our claim smokey smiled and said OK and if you might of found something can I ask how much you might of found Jim said I might of found 40 bars at 20 smokey reached for his calculator and after a minute he said that would be 16 million 863 thousand and 16 Sam looked at Jim and said if a man found that much could you afford that much smokey* said we'll and he looked at Earl and earl said yes we can together Jim said we'll I see Earl said what's it say on the bars Sam said CSA Earl just smiled smokey said if you have it and want to sell it the government don't need to know anything about it I'll just write it off as gold ore how's that sound. Jim said can you get to bank checks for 8 million 431 thousand before banks close smokey said can you have the gold here in a hour Jim said we will see you in little while smokey smiled and said OK let's go Earl Sam said we will be back in hour. Sam and Jim went back to Jim's place and dug the gold up they put it in the wagon and went back to the assay *office the seen that smokey was back the walked inside and smokey said did you bring it Sam said it's right out side he said come on Jim let's get it they carried the box inside and set it down smokey looked at the box it's in a old shipping box Jim said hat ain't all he popped the lid and reached in and handed the old colt to smokey that was in the box when we opened it along with this news paper smokey and Earl just stared at it then they reached it and took a gold bar out the said oh the stories this bar can tell it was right there during the Civil War Earl said you hoping in the colt Sam said sure Earl handed Sam the bank check and* smokey handed Jim his, Jim said well thanks a lot fellas you need us to move that for you they said know we got a dolly we can move it with Sam said we got a long ride back to the claim we got to get some supplies first Sam said we will be back next time when we're in town smokey said OK you boys don't be strangers Jim said we won't and they shook hands and walked out and got on there horses and went down by the bank the seen the Manger when they went in he said back so soon Jim said we need to deposit some big checks he said I'll help you out Jim said I just want to put mine in my account Sam said me to Jim handed the Manger *his check and said oh my your the reason smokey was in here to get this OK no problem he deposited it and gave Jim his receipt Sam handed him his and he said very good and in a few minutes he handed Sam his receipt and said you gentleman have a great day they walked out of the bank and rode down toward the supplies store before long the were ready to leave town Jim said it will be late when we get back what you say we stop and have us a home cook meal at the diner Sam said your reading my mind they rode the horse around back and tied them and walked inside and had a big dinner then they rode back toward the claim Sam said did you think it would turn out like this Jim looked up and said I didn't and I sure appreciate you including me in your claim Sam said I wanted someone I could trust and I new you would work hard Jim said well I thank you Sam said your welcome as the rode on in to the evening Jim said lets got see how much more gold we can find Sam said mi ready buddy.*